HILLEL BUILDS A HOUSE

To all the children of the Diaspora Yeshiva Day School
and especially to Yosef, who likes to build houses.
—S.L.

KAR-BEN PUBLISHING®
An imprint of Lerner Publishing Group, Inc.
241 First Avenue North
Minneapolis, MN 55401 USA

Website address: www.karben.com

Main body text set in Avenir LT Pro Roman.
Typeface provided by Linotype HG.

Library of Congress Cataloging-in-Publication Data

Names: Lepon, Shoshana, author. | Ruiz, Ángeles, 1971– illustrator.
Title: Hillel builds a house / by Shoshana Lepon ; illustrations by Ángeles Ruiz.
Description: Minneapolis, MN : Kar-Ben Publishing, [2020] | Series: [Sukkot &
    Simchat Torah] | Summary: A young boy who loves to build houses learns that
    the perfect holiday for him is Sukkot. Includes glossary. | Audience: Ages
    4–9. (provided by Kar-Ben Publishing.) | Audience: Grades K–1. (provided by
    Kar-Ben Publishing.) | Description based on print version record and CIP data
    provided by publisher; resource not viewed.
Identifiers: LCCN 2019042913 (print) | LCCN 2019042914 (ebook) |
    ISBN 9781541599604 (ebook) | ISBN 9781541544024 (library binding) |
    ISBN 9781541544031 (paperback)
Subjects: | CYAC: Fasts and feasts—Judaism—Fiction. | Sukkot—Fiction. |
    House construction—Fiction. | Jews—United States—Fiction.
Classification: LCC PZ7.L5555 (ebook) | LCC PZ7.L5555 Hi 2020 (print) |
    DDC [E]—dc23

LC record available at https://lccn.loc.gov/2019042913
LC record available at https://lccn.loc.gov/2019042914

Manufactured in the United States of America
1-45441-39687-3/30/2020

HILLEL BUILDS A HOUSE

Shoshana Lepon

illustrations by Ángeles Ruiz

KAR-BEN
PUBLISHING

"**WHERE IS HILLEL?**" his father asked. "I haven't seen him all afternoon. It's time to light the Hanukkah candles."

"In his room," answered his mother.

"Here I am," said Hillel. "I was in my room building another house!"

Hillel loved building houses.

Last summer, he built a tree house in the old oak out back with his dad.

When the days got chilly, Hillel made a new house under the basement steps.

Now even the basement was too cold.
Hillel dragged a large cardboard box upstairs
to his room. This would be his winter house.

His parents found Hillel with the box. He had made it into a house and was setting up his menorah.

"I'm going to celebrate Hanukkah in my new house!" Hillel declared.

"Your house is great," said his mother. "But you can't light candles in it."

"Why not?" asked Hillel.

"Because you might start a fire," his mother answered. "Besides, we light the menorah in the window so everyone will know about the miracle of Hanukkah."

Hillel moved his menorah down to the living room.

"Next holiday," he said to himself, "I'll celebrate in my very own house!"

Soon it would be Purim.

Hillel's friends were going to dress up in costumes. They would go from house to house and give out baskets of treats called *mishloach manot*.

Hillel thought and thought.
Suddenly he had an idea.

He would not stay home in his house.
He would take his house outside with him.
He would dress up as a house for Purim!

Hillel cut and glued and painted.
At last his costume was ready.

The pointy roof would rest on his
head. He made a small window in front
so he could see, and bigger windows
at the sides for his arms.

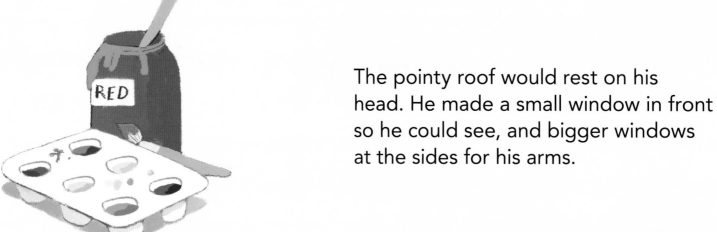

On Purim morning, Hillel got up early. He put on his house and hurried outside.

He could not see the sky overhead.

He could not see the dark clouds.

But he could feel the raindrops.

Soon his house was a mess of soggy cardboard!

Hillel ran home to change. He put on the space suit he had worn last year. He put his raincoat over it and went back outside.

"Next holiday . . ." he sighed.

The next holiday was Passover.

Hillel was excited. He went from room to room, gathering all the pillows he could find. He piled them into a snug little fort. "I'll play in here the whole week of Passover," he decided.

But his mother thought differently.

"Hillel," she said, "you have to take your house apart. We're having lots of guests, and we need the pillows. At the seder, we lean back like kings and queens to show that we are free!"

Hillel helped his mother put the pillows on the dining room chairs. "Next holiday . . ." he whispered to himself.

Spring arrived. It was warm and sunny outside.

Hillel tied some old sheets together and raised them on a pole in the backyard. He took out his sleeping bag.

"Tonight is Shavuot," he said. "I'll sleep out under the stars. I'll be like the Jews sleeping in the desert when they got the Torah at Mt. Sinai!"

"You won't be sleeping out here tonight, Hillel," said his father. "In fact, you won't be sleeping at all. Tonight we go to the synagogue. We stay up all night and study Torah. This year, you're old enough to come along."

Hillel was excited. He had never stayed up all night!

"Next holiday . . ." he promised himself.

On Rosh Hashanah, Hillel sat quietly beside his father in the synagogue. He liked the songs. But the prayers were long, and Hillel was getting tired.

He curled up in his seat and pulled one end of his father's tallit over his head. It made a nice little house.

He would rest his eyes for a minute . . .

"Hillel! Hillel!" His father shook him gently.
"Wake up! It's time to hear the shofar."

Hillel peered out from under the tallit.

Rosh Hashanah was no time for sleeping.

And it was no time for houses.

Yom Kippur was no time for houses, either. Hillel didn't need anyone to tell him that.

He would not fast all day like the grown-ups, but he would go to synagogue. And he would try to follow along in his prayer book.

When Hillel got home from synagogue,
the sky was filled with stars.

"Please get a flashlight, Hillel," said his father.
"I want you to help me with something."
Hillel followed his father out to the tool shed.

"Shine the light up here," said his father. "I have to take down some boards."

"What do you need boards for?" asked Hillel.

"Do you know what the next holiday is?" his father asked. "It's Sukkot! It's time to start building our sukkah. For seven days we'll eat outside under the stars, like the Jews who came out of Egypt."

"Sukkot!" exclaimed Hillel. "How could I have forgotten? Sukkot means hammers and nails and branches and fruits and lots of decorations."

"SUKKOT IS THE PERFECT TIME TO BUILD A HOUSE!"

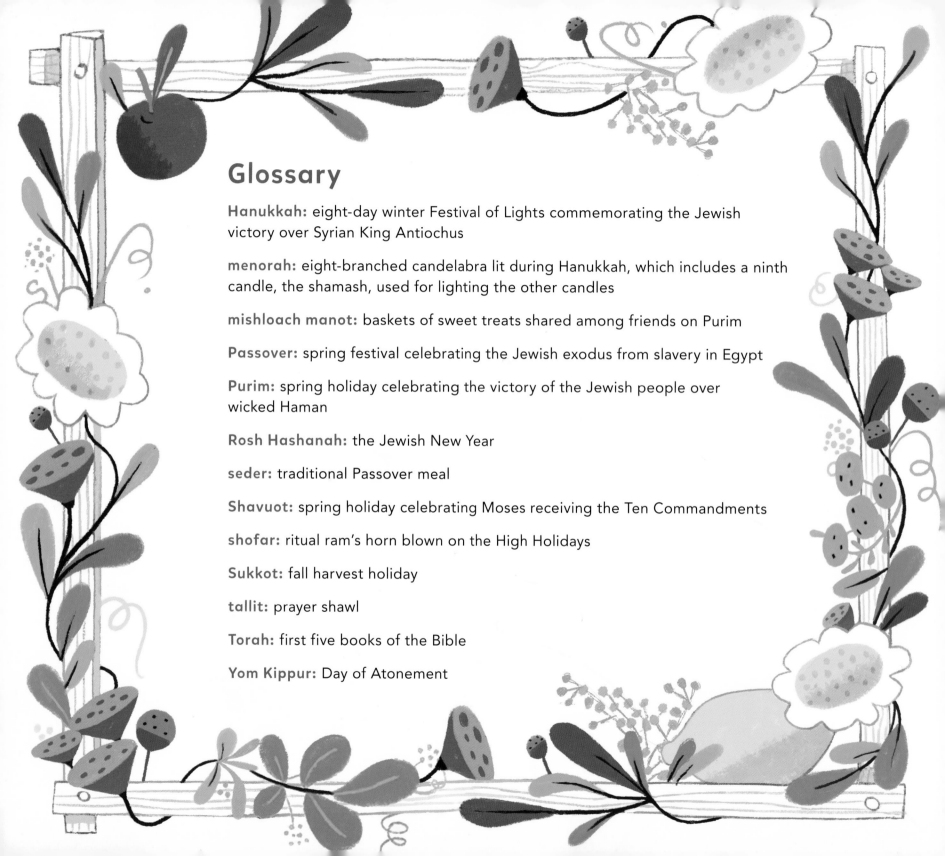

Glossary

Hanukkah: eight-day winter Festival of Lights commemorating the Jewish victory over Syrian King Antiochus

menorah: eight-branched candelabra lit during Hanukkah, which includes a ninth candle, the shamash, used for lighting the other candles

mishloach manot: baskets of sweet treats shared among friends on Purim

Passover: spring festival celebrating the Jewish exodus from slavery in Egypt

Purim: spring holiday celebrating the victory of the Jewish people over wicked Haman

Rosh Hashanah: the Jewish New Year

seder: traditional Passover meal

Shavuot: spring holiday celebrating Moses receiving the Ten Commandments

shofar: ritual ram's horn blown on the High Holidays

Sukkot: fall harvest holiday

tallit: prayer shawl

Torah: first five books of the Bible

Yom Kippur: Day of Atonement